The COMEDY of JOHN SEVERIN

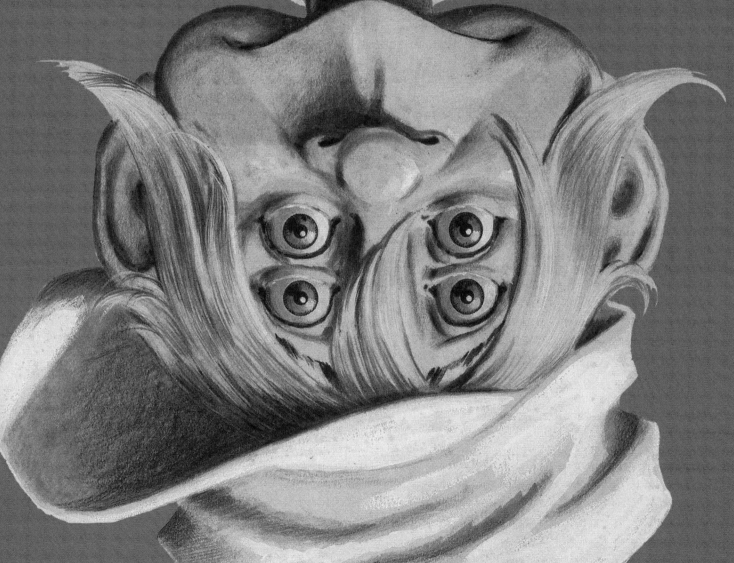

FUN IDEAS PRODUCTIONS
COMICFIX

SEVERIN

THE COMEDY OF JOHN SEVERIN

MORT TODD
Editor

MARK ARNOLD
Associate Editor

CHET "JASPER" REAMS
Contributing Editor

CLIFF MOTT
Original Reprint Art Director

SYLVESTER P. SMYTHE
Janitor

Dedicated to all the writers, artists, art directors, editors and publishers who kept Cracked magazine alive for so long!

Volume 1. Published by FUN IDEAS PRODUC-
TIONS & COMICFIX, an imprint of MORT
TODD LLC, POB 5392, Portland, Maine, 04101.
Names, characters and institutions used here are
fictitious and any similarity to actual people or
places is coincidental. No infringement of existing
trademarks or copyrights is intended or inferred,
and any use is for historic and educational purposes
under "fair use" terms of U.S. Code: Title 17, Sec.
107. Cracked is a trademark of Scripps Media, Inc.,
which has renounced any connection to the magazine, its contents and characters, except for its logo
and any limited use herein is for historical purposes. All remastered content © Comicfix. All
rights reserved. No part of this book may be repro-
duced in any form, except for newspaper, magazine
or Internet reviewers who quote passages or images
in connection with a review.

E-mail: comicfix@morttodd.com
Web: www.morttodd.com

The COMEDY of JOHN SEVERIN

INTRODUCTION by Mark Arnold

The opportunity to work on an actual *Cracked* magazine-related publication is a very exciting one for me. When my books *If You're Cracked, You're Happy, Volumes Won* and *Too* came out in 2011, I had no idea that anyone had any interest in *Cracked* anymore. I had gotten the assignment in 2009 by my publisher, BearManor Media, to which I responded with those immortal words, "Does anyone really care?" I have discovered since that people do care, care a lot, and even more so to this day, and that some people *Good Lord! Choke!* actually *preferred Cracked* over *Mad*.

For a magazine that had such a consistent release schedule for 46 years, from 1958-2004, it is almost unfathomable to think that *Cracked* no longer exists on the newsstands; the original run folding after 365 issues. Three more issues came out in 2007 by a different owner that bore little resemblance to what had come before and were quickly forgotten. After their failure, *Cracked* continued on as a successful, but again very different website that inspired a couple of books more in tune with the website.

As for myself, I got into *Mad* first. My sister, Carolyn, discovered the crazy artwork of Don Martin gracing the cover of *Mad Super Special* #14, and showed it to me one day in the grocery store in 1974. I was 7 years old. I went to my mom and asked if we could purchase it and my mom paid the 75¢ to get it for us. I was hooked, but didn't actually purchase another *Mad* until #172, January 1975, reading the remaining 1974 *Mad* issues in my local barber shop every time I went, until they were either taken by customers or thrashed so much that the barber finally had to throw them away.

My first exposure to *Cracked* was a slightly different experience. I believe I did see issue #115, March 1974 on the stands and was immediately turned off by the severed hand depicted in the M*A*S*H parody. Besides, I didn't think it was nearly as funny as *Mad*. The actual first issue of *Cracked* I purchased was #125, July 1975. I saw it in the same grocery store as I saw that first *Mad Super Special* a year before and like that experience, burst out laughing at what I saw in that issue. I later discovered that *Cracked* started hiring some better writers around that time.

I wasn't a *Cracked* convert as quickly as I had become a *Mad* one. I would get bored with *Cracked* and stop buying for awhile. Besides, there was also *Sick, Crazy* and *National Lampoon* on the stands to contend with and as a pre-teen and teenager, I only had so much spending money for such garbage. I summed these magazines up like this: *Mad* - good writing, good art; *Cracked* - bad writing, good art; *Crazy* - good writing, bad art; *Sick* - bad writing, bad art. *National Lampoon* - it really didn't matter, it had naked breasts in it! Actually, it had pretty good writing and artwork, too.

As a result of these conclusions, *Mad, Crazy* and *National Lampoon* were must buys. Sometimes I missed *Lampoon* because of the price, which was double that of *Mad* and the others, or if grandma objected too much. I managed to obtain it quite easily for a couple years until they slapped a "For Adults" on the cover in 1980, so I had to stop buying it for a few years.

Sick also ended in 1980 and *Crazy* in 1983, and I was prevented from buying *Lampoon* as stated, so after fitfully stopping and starting *Cracked* purchasing, I finally became a regular buyer in 1981. I was still annoyed with *Cracked* until Mort Todd took over the editorial reigns in 1985. As *Cracked* artist and writer Dan Clowes exclaimed, "No one was ever a fan of *Cracked*. We would buy *Mad* every month, but about two weeks later, we would get anxious for new material. We would tell ourselves, 'Ok, we are not going to buy *Cracked*. Never again!' And we'd hold out for a while, but then as the month dragged on, it just became, 'Ok f--- it, I guess I'll buy *Cracked*.' Then you'd bring it home, and immediately you'd remember, 'Oh yeah, I *hate Cracked*!'"

Oh, I remember now. This is supposed to be an introduction to **The Comedy of John Severin**, not my autobiography. Most of this material comes from *Giant Cracked* #46 (January 1987) one of the many, many reprint annuals and specials that *Cracked* published over the years, debuting in 1965. Until Mort Todd came along in 1985, most of these annuals were not very remarkable; just standard reprints from a few years back, plus some lame insert that had only the distinguishing characteristic of being printed on yellow paper. They never came close to the full-color, glossy and sometimes playable or lickable inserts that Mad had in their Specials. Mort Todd took these reprints to the next level by devising some sort of a theme, be it a subject like monsters, TV or movies, or promoting the value of some of Cracked's most-celebrated artists like John Severin or Jack Davis (see our companion volume **The Comedy of Jack Davis**).

Much has been written about John Powers Severin (December 26, 1921 - February 12, 2012), and extensive interviews conducted with the man appeared in *The Comics Journal* and other publications. Strangely, precious little was said or written in these interviews about Severin's tenure at *Cracked*

Mark Arnold is a comic book, animation and pop culture historian, who has written various books and articles about Harvey Comics, Underdog, The Beatles, Archie Comics, Disney, Pink Panther, The Monkees, Alvin and the Chipmunks, as well as *Cracked* Mazagine.

which spanned a longer time and greater amount of issues than anything he ever did for EC Comics on *Two-Fisted Tales*, *Frontline Combat* or *Mad*, or for Marvel Comics with *The Incredible Hulk*, *Conan the Barbarian*, *Sgt. Fury*, *Captain Savage* and *Kull*, or his extensive war and western work for Prize Comics and other publishers.

I first discovered Severin's artwork at *Cracked* and knew nothing of his previous art pedigree. I just figured *Cracked* was all he did. I was pleasantly surprised time and again at the astounding output of the man. Even when I tried to interview him for my *Cracked* books in 2010, Severin was still busy at work at age 88, turning out a brand-new *Bat Lash* story for DC Comics. I ended up interviewing Severin's charming wife, Michelena, who advised me that she knew more about his career than he did. She was right.

For most of his years at *Cracked*, Severin took a regular salary and also had the ability to draw as many pages as he wanted to while at *Cracked*. He took full advantage of this situation by literally drawing 50 out of 52 pages for *Cracked* #26, September 1962. These were the reasons as to why Severin had no interest in returning to *Mad*. (Severin did appear in the first 10 issues of *Mad*, edited by Harvey Kurtzman, before moving on to *Two-Fisted Tales* full-time.) There was also the sobering fact that Severin and second *Mad* editor Al Feldstein were not particularly fond of each other, to put it mildly.

Severin appeared in *Cracked* uninterrupted from 1958-1985, and it is this period where most of the material from this special *Giant Cracked* issue derives, mainly focusing on material from 1958-1969. After some savvy negotiating from Mort Todd, Severin returned to *Cracked* after being absent for a few issues and stayed almost to the final issue when money and anthrax problems derailed *Cracked* and led to its eventual demise. (The full details of this story are disclosed in my two-volume history, which also has a complete checklist of every *Cracked* issue.)

Mort and I hope you enjoy **The Comedy of John Severin**. John Severin is greatly missed, but through this volume, you can once again discover what it was that made John Severin truly great.

-Mark Arnold

Cracked veterans Mort Todd & John Severin created a daily newspaper comic strip called *Celebrity Biografix*. As a birthday surprise, Mort got Sev's friend, fellow comics legend and *Cracked* contributor Russ Heath to draw John's life story!

Celebrity Biografix ©morttodd.com

THE $64,000,000 CRACKED-POT QUESTION

Before I ask the second part, here's a tip for all you ladies. REVLOON, the nail polish for you, is so easy to put on. And when you want to remove it, simply apply a little turpentine, and sandpaper off. I use it myself everyday.

AROUND 'N' AROUND SHE GOES 'N' WHERE SHE STOPS NOBODY KNOWS

Now for part two, Squirt. "Whose picture appears on the dollar bill of Lower Slobovia?" Think carefully, and don't let anything distract you.

DUM·DUM DUM·DUM DUM·DUM DUM·DUM

I've got it. The answer is... 'MIKE RASPUTNIK.'

Oh, no.

ALWAYS WRITE BACKWARDS

SOLITARY CELL

I... I'm sorry, kid, but the answer is "JOE RASPUTNIK." "MIKE" appears on an UPPER Slobovia buck. Gee, kid, what can I say? It tears my heart to see you lose the loot.

BAW!

Sob, sob, I'm truly sorry, sonny, but I think we can scrape up some kind of consolation prizes for you.

WAAAAAA!

Sob... We'll give you Niagra Falls (with water). Also a Cinemascoped T.V. set, a bison, Miss Afghanistan, a car tank, a real Sputnik, a slightly used barber chair, half of Texas, a gold mine, and a few more small items, sob.

Baw! I want the cash!

BUS STOP

—a tale so miserable—

IT SHOULDN'T HAPPEN TO A DOG

... An' I'm jush the (Hiccup!) dog they have in mind, bartender. Thash right, little old me!

Me, the greatesh TALKING DOG there ever was. Any other mutt with my talent ... He'd be sitting right there on top of the world.

You know why? 'Cause he'd be tied up with somebody who could sell him. You know wha' I'd be if I had an agent who knew the right people an' how to talk to them ...?

... I'd be the biggesh star Hollywood ever had!

... I'd (Hiccup!) be the biggesh star TV ever had!

Wouldn't I? The greatesh talking dog there ever was, wouldn't I? If only I was tied up with somebody who could talk to the right people, instead of with thish lunkhead!

WURRF! WURRF!

... All HE can do is just bark!

This is the picture they DARED them to make. Yes, this is the English picture the English dared them to make in Ireland. However, that great English producer J. Arthur Crank proved he wasn't chicken and made the picture anyway. As he later said from his hospital bed . . . . "Blimey, it was worth it." CRACKED'S reviewer gives it 4 stars . . . . for guts.

J. ARTHUR CRANK

PRESENTS . . . .

'ENRY 'IGGINS OF SCOTLAND YARD

in living colorless
starring

SIR REX 'ARRISON
SIR CEDRIC 'ARDRICK
SIR 'ARDRICK SHMENDRICK
LADY SHIRLEY YIMAGOOTCHIE
(as the girl)

An English speaking picture
with American titles

NARRATED BY
ROCKY GRAZIANO

FINANCED BY
THE ROYAL BANK

MUSIC BY THE
ROYAL GLEE CLUB

ESCAPED THROUGH THE
LONDON UNDERGROUND

SEVERIN

H'I'VE A SUSPICION OF FA-OWL PLYE 'ERE. 'N' H'AIN'T NOBODY TER TUCH A BLOODY THING.

RIGHT YER BE H'INSPECTOR.

'AVE 'NOTHER CUHP H'INSPECTOR . . . . CLEARS THE CRANNY FER CLEWS.

THENKS, SMIRCHBOTTOM. HI SIGH, HANY BUTLERS 'ANGING 'BOUT THE PREMISES?

A FEW H'INSPECTOR 'IGGINS, BUT HI SURSPECK H'OV THEIR HINNOCENCE.

'AVE YER SEARCHED THE PLICE . . . . ARE YER CERTAIN THERE BE NO HUPSTAIRS MIDES 'IDIN DOWNSTAIRS?

POISON

✗ Somethin' screwy's goin' on here. You guys keep yer cottin' pickin' hands off.

✗ Yeah.

✗ Dis'll make ya tink better, chief.

✗ Let's pin it on the butler.

✗ Got nuttin' on him, chief.

✗ Dere must be a dame in the case. Go find me a maid.

*Inspector, here's the maid you wanted.
+MARONE! WOW!

*I hafta ask ya a few questions, baby.
+Go on, copper, but I ain't done nuttin'!

*The poor kid.
+Know any of these jokers, honey?

*Vaguely.
+Take notes, Smirchbottom.

*I found a new suspect.
+First I've gotta make a full report on 'er.

*This guy's confessed.
+The Yard must investigate further.

*It could be that HE did it.
+The Yard leaves nuttin' to chance.

*It's the duty of the Yard to look into this.

*Bury him in the Yard.

x Go get the birds together so's I can close this miserable case. x Awright

x Here's a character we can pin it on.

x Couldn't be him, he's a deadhead.

x I got 'm all rounded up.

x Here's how I figure it. One guy here is guilty just like in the movies.
x And I'm smart enough to know who the rat is.

x There's no loot involved, since this guy is busted." Get to the pernt, who did it?

x This is the guy. He's been fakin' it.
x You don't say so?

x What a stupid ending. I ain't gonna bother even to explain it.

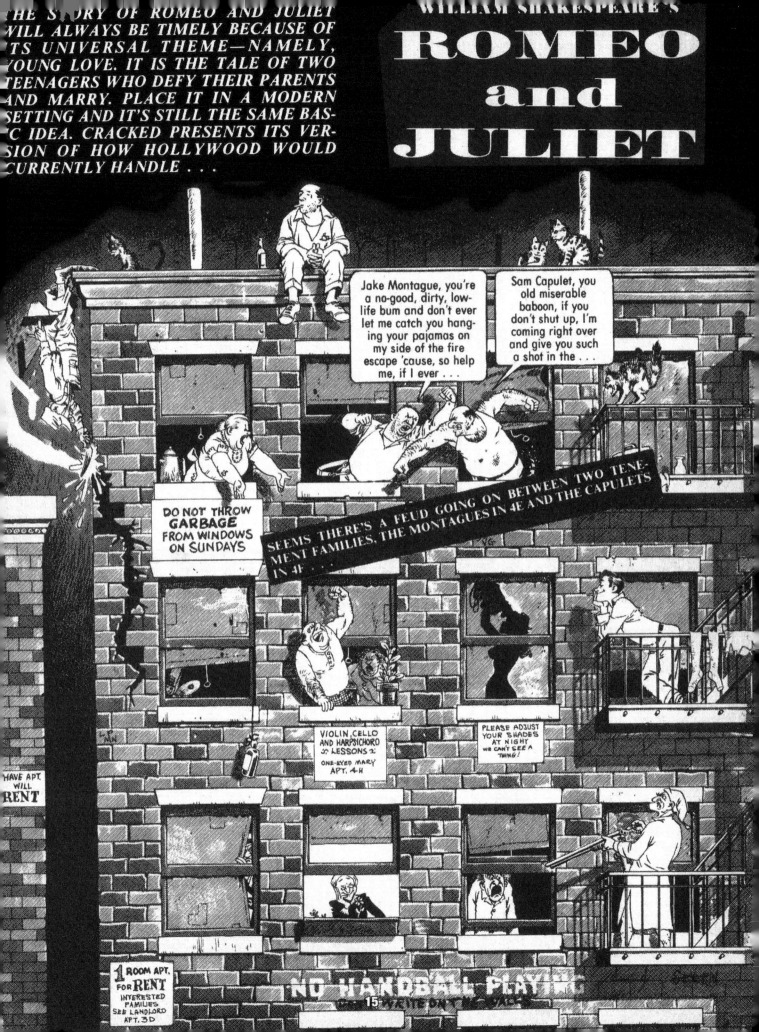

ALASKA, NEW FRONTIER OF GOLDEN OPPORTUNITIES

When a new frontier opens, it offers tremendous opportunities to the courageous and the enterprising. Alaska is no exception! Here are some of the opportunities that await those who venture into its virgin territory!

WEALTH. YOU CAN MAKE A FORTUNE IN ALASKA, BY MARRYING A RICH WIDOW.

HEALTH. THE CRISP, COOL AIR IS HEALTHFUL. JUST BRING PLENTY OF COLD TABLETS

OBSCURITY. ON THE LAM? ALASKA IS A GREAT PLACE TO HIDE OUT!

Criminal-shriminal. It's T-TOO C-COLD! L-let's go home!

DULL ALASKAN STATISTICS

Alaska has 6 mountain ranges! For the lazy climber, we recommend the Kloddy Mountains, only sixteen inches high!

Alaska's greatest river is the Yukon. It is very popular with tourists because it is filled with beer instead of water.

The Koyukyok flows south from the Brooks Bros. Hills, into the Yonkil Basin, and onto a three inch beach.

HELP! I'm FALLING!

This cold competition with Texas is unfair!

And it's also unfair to SCHLEMIEL'S BEER!

COLD SHOULDER FRIGID ALASKA

PATRONIZE HOT Passionate TEXAS

ALASKA'S IMPACT ON OUR CULTURE

New T.V. show, "THE LONE ALASKAN" tops all ratings, even Desilulus', "I LOVE ALASKA."

New Alaskan Rock 'N' Roll tune smashes all records of all time histories.

Stylish women formerly wore sack dresses; now wear ghastly Alaskan-style dresses.

Tourists, bored with Florida, Las Vegas, and California, flock to our new state.

Comedians, hard up for jokes, are saved at the last minute by our 49th state.

Texans get inferiority complexes.

Almost everybody is happy about it except the husband of a certain little old lady.

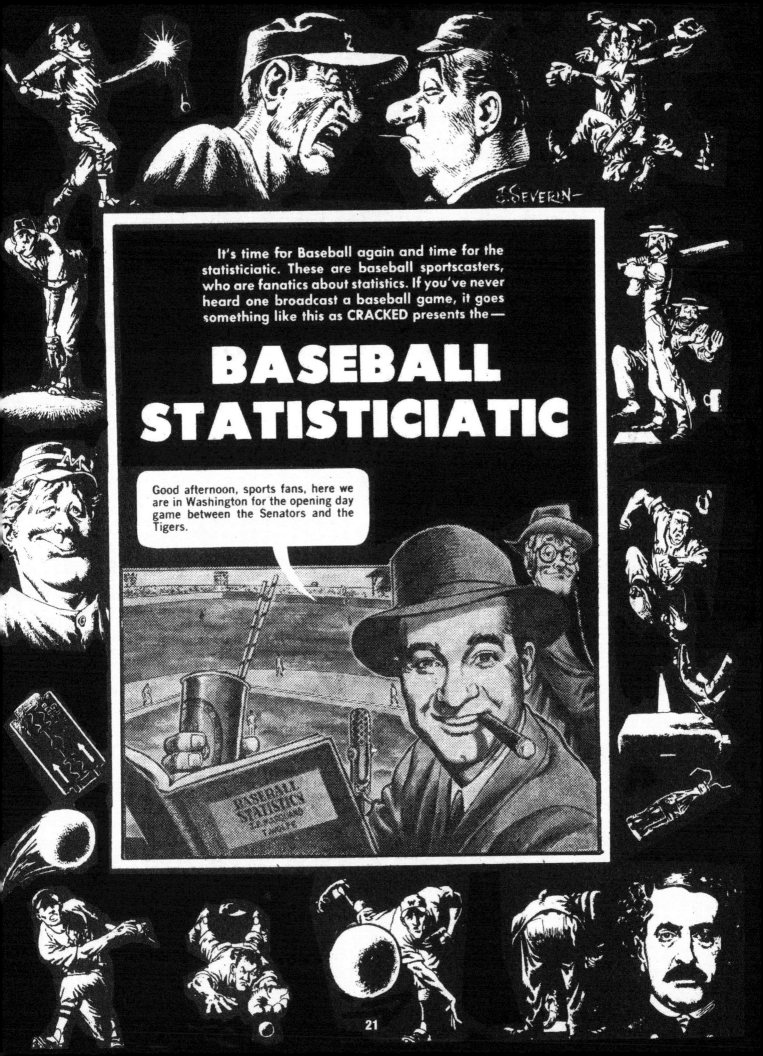

It's time for Baseball again and time for the statisticiatic. These are baseball sportscasters, who are fanatics about statistics. If you've never heard one broadcast a baseball game, it goes something like this as CRACKED presents the—

BASEBALL STATISTICIATIC

Good afternoon, sports fans, here we are in Washington for the opening day game between the Senators and the Tigers.

It's a beautiful day here in Washington. But it is raining in Detroit. This is the third year in succession that it has been rain- ing in the visitors' hometown on an open- ing day away game. These two ball clubs are meeting for the sixth time in an open- ing day game. Detroit has won three and Washington has won two. In the 1938 season opener the game was rained out

an interesting item. There are two grand- fathers on the Washington team; there are 21 fathers who have 41 children, 24 boys and 17 girls. . . . Oh, here's a correc- tion fans. I was wrong, it did rain in De- troit on opening day of the 1938 season. So it was raining in both cities—you can make that correction if any of you are keeping statistics at home. Wait a minute

which team is ahead? Well, no one in the press box seems to have that information, but we're sending someone out to ask a fan in the stands. The pressbox is just 100 feet from the first row in the stands. We are exactly 215 feet above the playing

here in Washington, interestingly enough it was sunny in Detroit on that day. The sun is shining from left field across third

base to the pitcher's mound. It is 45 feet from 3rd base to the pitcher's mound. It is 90 feet from the pitcher's mound to

home plate, 60 feet from batter's box to the dugout and 75 feet from the Press booth to the refreshment stand. Here's

fans, I think it's starting to rain here, fans. If rain should cancel this game, it would be the first opening day game rained out

after it began. One game was halted in 1937 but that was due to a snowstorm. Since this game has gone more than four

and a half innings, the team ahead at the time the game is called, would be declared the winner. Does anyone know

field. By the way, what's the score Joe? 23 boys and 15 girls? That's the number

of children on the washington team. Oh well, the score doesn't matter, it's how

you play the game that counts. So until tomorrow, friends, keep drinking and smoking…it makes for happier sponsors.

Are you nervous? Unhappy? Miserable? This could mean you're in love. This could also mean you've been reading the articles up 'till now. Any way you look at it, both can be painful ordeals. To determine whether you're in love, or just a miserable clod, take this test and you will soon find out . . .

SCORE
THIS WAY

TRUE 15 points
COULD BE 10 points
MAYBE 5 points
FALSE 0 points

AM I

You can't eat.

You can't sleep.

You can't seem to concentrate on your work.

You're awkward and clumsy whenever she's around.

You find yourself speechless in her presence.

You get burning sensations when she's near you.

You just can't live without her.

You feel like running thru the streets shouting.

Mostly you feel like you're just plain nauseous.

REALLY IN LOVE?

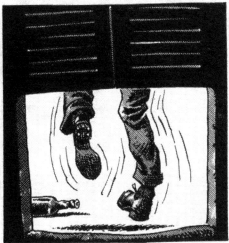

Sometimes you feel like you're walking on air.

You see her high on a pedestal.

You get goose pimples when she enters the room.

You're hurt by her slightest rejection.

Your heart feels like it's on fire.

You're terrified at first meeting her parents.

NOW ADD UP YOUR SCORE AND SEE JUST WHERE YOU STAND ON CUPID'S LADDER

20	40	60	80	100	120	140	160	180
YOU'RE HOPELESSLY IN LOVE	YOU'RE ALMOST IN LOVE	YOU'RE SLIGHTLY IN LOVE	YOU'RE NOT IN LOVE	YOU DON'T EVEN LIKE THE GIRL	YOU HATE THE GIRL	THE GIRL HATES YOU	YOU HATE YOURSELF	WE HATE YOU

An Introvert likes to be by himself. An Extrovert likes to mix with other people. To determine just how far out YOU are, take this simple test, and . . .

RATE YOUR

ARE YOU AN INTROVERT?

Do you brood inwardly over every little thing?

Yes [ ]   No [ ]

Do you seem unable to function well in groups?

Yes [ ]   No [ ]

Do you have difficulty relating to strangers?

Yes [ ]   No [ ]

Do you hate intrusion of others on your privacy?

Yes [ ]   No [ ]

Do you feel inhibited in releasing your emotions?

Yes [ ]   No [ ]

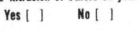

Do you dislike being the center of attraction?

Yes [ ]   No [ ]

Do you feel nervous and uneasy moving in crowds?

Yes [ ]   No [ ]

Do people have to coax you into joining the fun?

Yes [ ]   No [ ]

SCORE YOURSELF

(Turn over on other side or stand on head to read)

take NO for an answer.
are really a sad case—'cause you don't
of these questions "YES," this means you
in a world by yourself. If you answered all
these questions "YES," this means you are
troverted personality. If you answered 5 of
"YES," this means you have a slightly in-
If you answered 3 of these questions

ARE YOU AN INTROVERT?

26

PERSONALITY
ARE YOU AN EXTROVERT?

Do you become restless when you're by yourself?

Yes [ ]　　　No [ ]

Do you usually seek to attract attention?

Yes [ ]　　　No [ ]

Do you insist on having an audience?

Yes [ ]　　　No [ ]

Do you seem to make friends easily?

Yes [ ]　　　No [ ]

Do you tend toward showing off at parties?

Yes [ ]　　　No [ ]

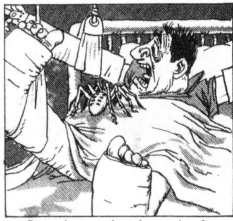

Do you always need people around you?

Yes [ ]　　　No [ ]

SCORE YOURSELF

(Turn over on other side or stand on head to read)

tions.

out—mainly because there are only 8 ques-

questions "YES," this means you are way

pretty far out. If you answered 9 of these

these questions "YES," this means you are

troverted personality. If you answered 5 of

"YES," this means you have a slightly ex-

If you answered 3 of these questions

ARE YOU AN EXTROVERT?

Do you have an open and assertive personality?

Yes [ ]　　No [ ]

27

Do you genuinely like to mix with people?

Yes [ ]　　　No [ ]

One of the more publicized figures today is, unquestionably, the one belonging to the French cinema star, Brigitte Bardot. With all the excitement she inspires, CRACKED got to wondering how she might look if some of the great artists of yesterday and today had painted her. So, like, with a little stretch of our imaginations, we can imagine.

BARDOT   *Amedeo Modigliani*

THE ARTIST'S SISTER   *James Whistler*

THE BIRTH OF VENUS   *Sandro Botticelli*

GIRL WITH TOWEL   *Pablo Picasso*

BRIGITTE BARDOT
as seen by different artists

UNFINISHED PORTRAIT   *Gilbert Stuart*

THE GIRL AT THE WINDOW   *Jan Vermeer*

THE DUCHESS DE BARDOT   *Francisco De Goya*

MAMA MIA! *Leonardo Da Vinci*

SUNFLOWER GIRL   *Vincent Van Gogh*

THERE ARE NO HANDS   *Dali*

AMERICAN GALLIC   *Grant Wood*

Today the big thing in humor is the "Sick Joke." Many people however, think that this is a recent phenomena in American culture. But like "Sick Jokes" are nothing new in our society.

The 'Little Willie' verses, written over fifty years ago, were really the very first "sick jokes." And so we thought maybe you'd like to hear what your grandparents used to laugh at, as CRACKED

ILLUSTRATED Little Willies

Little Willie hung his sister;
She was dead before we missed her.
"Willie's always up to tricks.
Ain't he cute? He's only six!"

Willie's cute as cute can be!
Beneath his brother, only three,
He lit a stick of dynamite.
Now Bubby's simply out of sight!

Willie split the baby's head,
To see if brains were grey or red.
Mother, troubled, said to father,
"Children are an awful bother!"

Little Willie, mirror gazer,
Found a use for papa's razor;
Sister razzed, "Too young to shave!"
Now they're digging sister's grave.

Willie and two other brats
Licked up all the Rough-on-rats.
Father said, when mother cried,
"Never mind—they'll die outside."

Willie on the railroad track—
The engine gave a squeal.
The engineer just took a spade
And scraped him off the wheel.

Into the well our little Willie
Pushed his baby sister Lily.
Mother couldn't find her daughter:
Now we sterilize our water.

Willie heard his sisters' scream,
So he threw them in the stream,
Saying, as he drowned the third,
"Children should be seen, not heard!"

Little Willie, with father's gun,
Punctured grandma, just for fun.
Mother frowned at the merry lad:
It was the last shell father had.

Pity now poor Mary Dillie.
Blinded by her brother Willie.
Red hot nails in her eyes he poked
I never saw Mary more provoked!

Willie poisoned his father's tea;
Father died in agony.
Mother came, and looked quite vexed:
"Really, Will," she said, "what next?"

Willie fell down the elevator—
Wasn't found till six days later.
Then the neighbors sniffed, "Gee whizz!
What a spoiled child Willie is!"

Willie in the cauldron fell;
See the grief on mother's brow!
Mother loved her darling well;
Darling's quite hard-boiled by now.

Willie saw some dynamite,
Couldn't understand it quite.
Curiosity never pays;
It rained Willie seven days.

Your OCEAN TRIP to Europe...
So Much More Than Transportation

Eager faces tell the story aboard an OCEAN ship crossing the Atlantic. Where else in the world can you experience such complete detachment from everyday problems? If you're going to Europe, an OCEAN crossing is ideal for those who can change their minds in the middle. You'll marvel at the luxurious, form-fitting Preservers, especially designed for that relaxed feeling while floating on the water. You'll experience new sensations as you are lowered into a well-appointed, custom-built lifeboat, complete with 14-day rations. So for something different in that ocean voyage, try an OCEAN Liner.

Getting half way there is fun ... Go **OCEAN**

Widest Choice of Preservers, Life Boats and Rafts from New York to Europe. Consult your Insurance Agent before you apply.

TITANIC • LUSITANIA • BISMARCK • ANDREA DORIA • MAINE

Recently we gave you all a chance to do your own art work in CRACKED by featuring Do-It-Yourself drawings. This was done mainly because our artist missed the deadline. Now we find we're stuck with a batch of drawings — and we can't find that idiotic writer! So like we're shoving it in anyway in order to give all you budding writers an opportunity to write for CRACKED. Just fill in the captions and mail 'em back to us. Who knows? Like Maybe we can discover some new clod — with these . . .

DO-IT-

YOURSELF CAPTIONS

With more and more women entering the business world each year, it's becoming increasingly difficult for men to find jobs. The result is that women are slowly taking over the position of family breadwinner. Naturally this has an affect on the home. Obviously this has an affect on family life. Mainly this has an affect on the sexes themselves. Which brings us to CRACKED's version of what may happen, if this keeps up, and...

how family life would be
IF THE SEXES CHANGED PLACES

Hello, dear. Have a nice day at the office?

Some day! I'm pooped! That Higgins' deal finally went through. I'm up for promotion. How'd your day go?

The baby was teething so I had to rush him to the doctor and almost missed my appointment at the barber. I do So want to look well for bridge at the Smedleys...

Darn it! I forgot all about the Smedleys tonight. I really don't feel like going, dear. You know how dull those bridge sessions get— with all that small talk...

There, there ... you just curl up in your easy chair and relax while I fix dinner. You'll feel better after you eat ..

Fine, honey. Say! What's for dinner tonight? (sniff sniff) HMMMMMMMM ... Smells good ...

I cooked you your favorite —beef stew.

Beef stew? That's marvelous, darling. I just love the way you make it.

THONK!

37

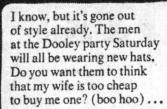

I know, but it's gone out of style already. The men at the Dooley party Saturday will all be wearing new hats. Do you want them to think that my wife is too cheap to buy me one? (boo hoo) . . .

Aw-ww! Cut the crying. You know I can't stand to see you cry. Isn't that just like a man? I'd like to know one thing. What do you do with all the money I give you??

The lousy fourteen bucks you bring me home? You think it's easy managing a household, buying groceries, washing and ironing, taking care of two small children, now another one on the way??

Whattaya mean? I know what you're doing! I work hard for my money. I bring it home and you throw it away on hats, mah jongg, luncheons.

You don't love me! Mother was right. I shoulda married Selma, the doctor. Or even Barbara, who makes a darn good living as a longshoreman! Oh, I shoulda married her when she asked me to. Instead I . . .

Now don't bring that up! I was a pretty dashing figure with the men and I could have fell in easy, Why I . . .

If that's the way you feel about it, we're through! I'm going home to Father . . .

Go ahead! Good riddance! It's the last time I'll try to argue logically with a man!

Stop shouting! The children will hear you! They're in the next room . . .

I AM NOT SHOUTING!!

Quiet!!! I think you did it! I hear them coming now . . .

Come in, kids, and say hello to your mommy . . .

Mommy! Buy me a bicycle for my birthday!!

Daddy! My dolly doesn't go ba-wa anymore!!

38

The gift of love . . .

·F·MᶜCUMAL·

A diamond is forever

Treasured moments of courtship burn with a stronger glow when brightened by a sparkling diamond. For lovers everywhere it is magic time and the world is alive with romance and the tender enchantment of a dream. Yet few people can tell the difference between a genuine diamond and a rhinestone. Why then, should you pay a fortune for a real diamond when you can pass off a cheap imitation and fool everybody. Remember . . . being passed off as genuine.

The gift of love . . . painted for the
De Queers collection by John Severin

HOW TO "PASS OFF" A DIAMOND
First, go buy a cheap rhinestone. Then get some ordinary glass polish and start shining it up. Soon it will begin to sparkle like the real thing. You can now give it to the one you love, who will never even know the difference. Unless the one you love happens to be a jewel-er, that is.

De Queers Rhinestone Co., Inc.

For all those who wrote in asking for more cultural articles and more imaginative shut-ups, we put the two together and now come up with . . .

SHAKESPEAREAN

SHUT-UPS

In keeping with our policy of introducing new and talented young artists to the public, CRACKED now opens up its pages to an exhibit of paintings by several of the country's most gifted, but unknown, painters. Any similarity between these paintings and any other living paintings, good or bad, is purely accidental—as we present . . .

A CRACKED GALLERY OF NEW ARTISTS

BALLET REHEARSAL IN STAGE DELICATESSEN
by
Edgar Deguts

STILL BLECH
by
Oswald Laino

DANCE AT BIRDLAND
by
Auguste Renoise

RUE TRANSNONAME
by
Henri Daumiechh

BLECHDAY
by
Marc Chaghoul

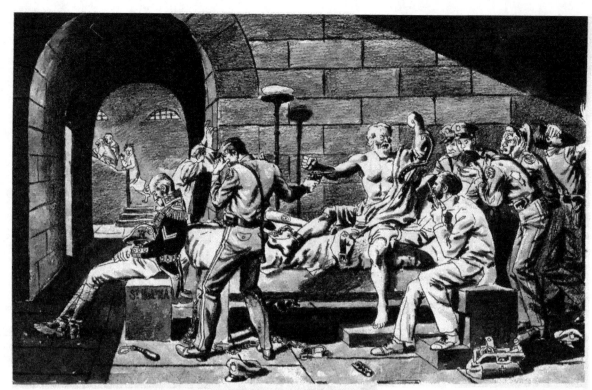

THE DILEMMA OF SOCRATES
by
Sylvester Davoid

THE STACKING OF CARDS
by
Paul Cezane

THE SCREECHING GYPSY
by
Henri Rousster

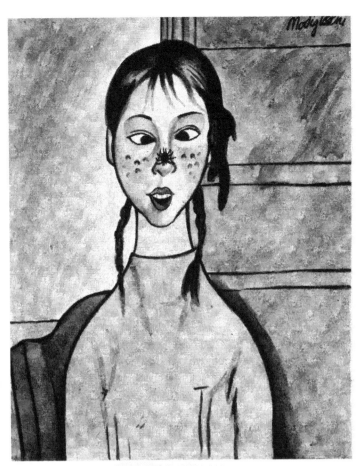

GIRL WITH BRAINS
by
Amadeo Modiglooni

THE FLUKEY REPAST
by
Pablo Picusso

RIFT OF THE MEDULLA
by
Max Gericlod

THE UNSOCIABLES *prefer Espresso*

SEVERIN-

THEY GO WHERE THE KICKS ARE—in their own private worlds. And ESPRESSO is always there. It fills without refreshing . . . this means you can live on ESPRESSO for days without eating—and also you won't get that square refreshed feeling. You can remain beat as you sip it. Today's hipsters prefer the drink that matches their static pace. Be one of THE UNSOCIABLES. Have an ESPRESSO anywhere—at a coffee shop, in your pad or at your favorite wild party.

Be Unsociable, Have an Espresso

STAY BEAT!
Fills without refreshing

"ESPRESSO" is a trademark of the Beatniks of America.

STORY OF THE MONTH

Imitation, the day people tell us, is the sincerest form of flattery. These same dingbats also insist that you can't kid a kidder—especially if he's a master at the game. Here Cracked's Crackedest Artist demonstrates his own fool-hardy brand of flattery in kidding a certain Madman who shall remain nameless . . .

AT THE ART GALLERY

CURVY SEWER COGNAC

What a host of historic binges are associated with this noble French Cognac! It is THE BRANDY of NAPOLEON.

For centuries, famous french generals and statesmen have enjoyed Curvysewer for it's **pour la gloire** flavor, and it's **pour la glow** kick.

The Brandy of Napoleon

From the famous Curvysewer collection of Napoleon paintings (Musee De Versalles)

Napoleon and staff sizing up the situation in anticipation of a slight skirmish, 1815.

Since Frank Sinatra and Gang had such a ball remaking "Gunga Din" into "Soldiers Three," we wondered what it would be like if they redid some major screen classics in their own inimitable concept of some . . .

CLAN CLINKERS

52

THE CLAN IN DRACULA

The sun is at last setting.

. . . it's time to arouse Count Dracula and his Bat Pack!

Oh, how I hate to see that evening sun go down.

RISE AND SHINE.

Let's go, gang! It's time to chew the fat with the local maidens!

Boss, look at that bevy of red-blooded Americans!

I'm going after pretty Shirley!

And I'll take sexy Kim!

I got lovely Liz!

Who have you got, Count Dino?

BLOODY MARY! (HIC!)

54

THE CLAN IN TARZAN OF THE APES

To prepare our children for the adult world they will have to face, we should present them with a more realistic view of our society. One way to do this is to introduce them to the modern tabloid newspaper through the medium of the familiar nursery-rhyme. For example, here is . . .

MOTHER GOOSE CONFIDENTIAL

Price: Sing a Song of Sixpence

Weather Outlook:
Rain, rain go away,
Come again
some other day.

Circulation: 3 (Wynken, Blynken and Nod)

ASPCA INVESTIGATES DOG NEGLECT CASE

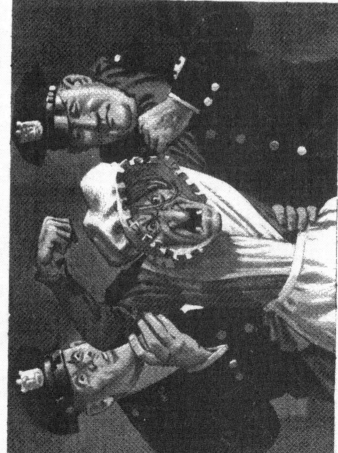

Authorities of the ASPCA this afternoon were busily studying a charge of canine negligence brought against Mother Hubbard, elderly suburban housewife. "It isn't my fault!" cried the old mother. "When I got to the cupboard, it was bare!"

FARMER'S WIFE RUNS AMUCK

CONTRARY TO RUMORS OFFBEAT BLONDE

WINS GARDEN SHOW

THREE MEN FOUND IN TUB

Members of the Sanitation Department last night rounded up three men who were found in a bathtub. They were identified as a butcher, a baker and a candlestick maker. "For the first time in our lives, we're really clean!" protested the baker in vain. The three were held without bail.

O SOLO MIO—It's my solo
TRES CHIC—Three chickens
ALOHA—I'll pay her back

LONDON BRIDGE ON VERGE OF COLLAPSE?

London.—Rumors concerning the shaky stability of famed old London Bridge were circulating freely through the city today following an insidious whisper campaign started by a gang of rowdies who serenaded their tow-headed female gangleader with the refrain: "London Bridge is falling down, my fair lady!"

JAZZ PIPER'S SON STEALS PIG

The ten-year-old son of a famed jazz clarinetist broke down today after repeated questioning by detectives and admitted that he was the one who stole the prize sow reported missing last week. Furthermore, the self-styled "pork addict" bragged of having barbequed his victim over a hickory fire. "Man, like I'm all hung up on ribs!" was his only comment to reporters.

GUTE TAG—Go to the dogs

IPSO FACTO—It's a fact

Dreaming of making a Christmas pie so savory that your family can't resist digging their thumbs in to snare the juicy plums? Then follow the advice of plum-diving, Champion Chef J. Horner who displays no false modesty over his culinary achievement. "What a good boy am I!" boasted the jovial epicure.

YOUNG MAN BRINGS DISCRIMINATION CHARGES

A wool—gathering teenager who asked that his name be withheld charged discrimination today in the distribution of three bags of wool from local sheep. He claimed the Master got one and some Dame got one, but due to prejudice, he received none. "Just because I was crying in the lane!" he sobbed. A full investigation is now being conducted by the Anti-Defamation League.

An attractive blonde named Mary brought something more than a green thumb to the Annual Flower Show and walked off with top honors. When asked how her garden grew, the eccentric beauty replied: "With cockle shells and silver bells and pretty maids all in a row." She was promptly rushed to the State Mental Hospital for observation.

HOUSING AUTHORITIES FIND FAMILY LIVING IN SHOE

A possible answer to the housing problem created by the population explosion was examined today by authorities who found an old woman and her family actually living in a shoe—and getting a boot out of it! The woman, who is sole owner of the dwelling, explained: "I have so many children I didn't know what to do!"

EXCLUSIVE!

Cafe International's madcap heir, Georgie-Porgie Puddinpy III, ran out of El Morocco after kissing seven post-debutantes until they cried. "Dot Georgie!" exclaimed playgirl Zu Zu Dabore, through painfully swollen lips. "Ven the girls decide they want to play, too —dot's ven he runs away!"

EGG HEAD FALLS FROM TERRACE WALL, DIES

Famed intellectual Humpty K. Dumpty fell from a perch fifty feet above a Brussels sidewalk in a suspected suicide leap. The King promptly sent all available horses and men in a futile attempt at reviving the victim. Friends reported Dumpty as complaining recently of "feeling rotten."

Hacks Tails Off 3 Mice

In a new outbreak of violence today, a farmer's wife suddenly went berserk and chopped off the tails of three blind mice with a large carving knife. Questioned by a psychiatrist, the attractive, blonde housewife stated that when they all ran after her, everything went black. "I never saw such a sight in my life!" cried an outraged onlooker.

UNE BELLE DIE—A nice funeral

SOUP DE JOUR—Feed the jury

In the words of the fabulously wealthy Chinese philosopher, Tai Koon, there is only one tragedy in life greater than not having your big dream come true— and that's having it coming true.

THE DREAM

Toiling under the hot sun
was Abner's lot in life.

Life's only comfort was the
thought of a distant retirement.

Unmercifully, the years drifted by
—all too slowly.

Poor Pvt. Bemish was always
taking orders.

If only he could become an officer,
the tables would be turned.

He applied for Officer Candidate School,
where he underwent the most gruelling
months of his life.

This hot oriental aphorism is coolly expressed by one of our coolie-artists in a series called . . .

CAME TRUE

Then one day, the dream came true!

. . . And Abner is still toiling under the hot sun.

Then one day, the dream came true!

. . . And Bemish is taking more orders than ever before.

Young Gladys was miserable. Her family was the poorest in the neighborhood.

She promised herself that she'd marry above her station.

To get the right man, she connived, she schemed and she coquetted.

George, a clerk, craved the finer things in life.

And he swore that he'd be a big success some day.

He worked his way untiringly up the ladder of success.

There wasn't much Harry could do to escape his fate— a west-side tenement.

But, by golly, his children were going to amount to something!

Simple pleasures were denied and every penny went toward the family goal.

Then one day, the dream came true!

. . . And her family is still the poorest in a neighborhood of millionaires!

Then one day, the dream came true!

VICE PRESIDENT

GEORGE T. SL

. . . And ulcer-plagued George is still craving.

And Harry's sophisticated beatnik kids returned to their old, authentic Bohemian tenement.

Then one day, the dream came true!

CRACKED LOOKS AT HUNTING AND FISHING

LePoer

"Hey, Joe . . . See·if you can **figure** these tracks out!"

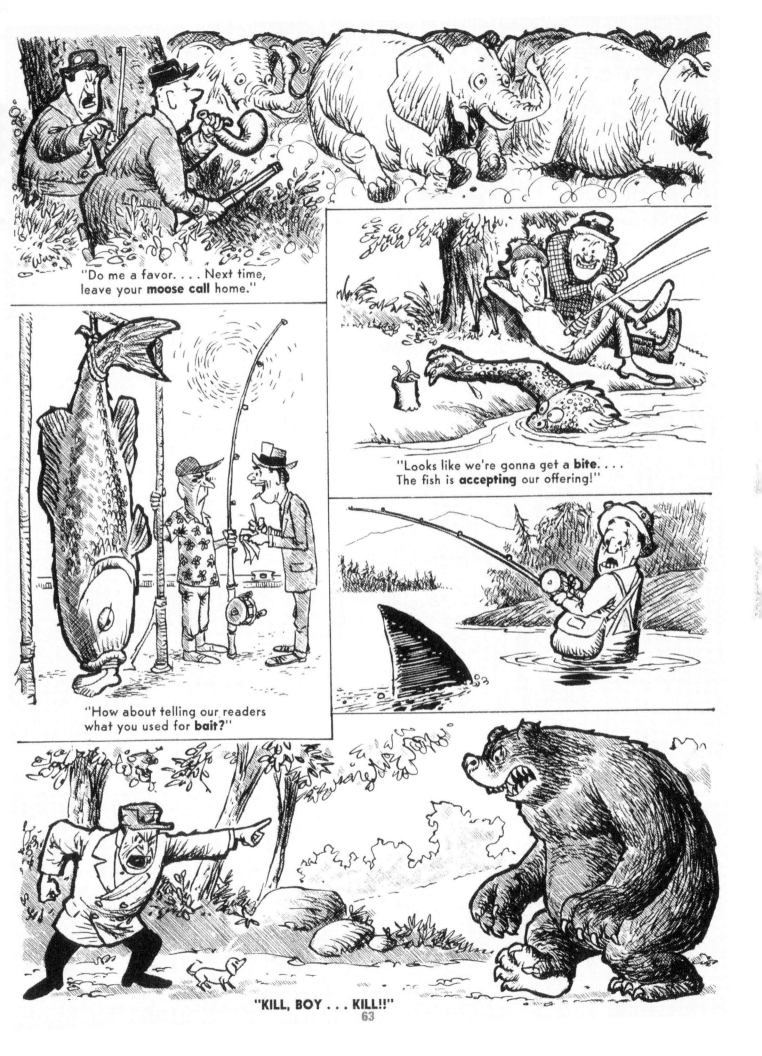

HURRY-UPS

In this issue, CRACKED introduces the latest fad. Hot on the heels of the Shup-Ups and the Wind-Up Dolls comes the HURRY-UP! Here is our contribution to the movement. How about you? Heard any good ones lately? If so, Hurry Up—and share them with us!

ONE OF THE MOST POPULAR NIGHT TIME TV PROGRAMS IS THE STEVE ALLEN SHOW.... CRACKED NOW TAKES A LOOK TO SEE WHAT MAKES IT A HUGE SUCCESS WITH ITS MILLIONS OF FANS....

THE STEVE ALLEN SHOW!

THE PROGRAM IS POPULAR BECAUSE OF CRAZY STUNTS STEVE DOES...

THE DIRECTOR'S OFF-CAMERA STUNTS ARE ZANY ...

FANS ENJOY WATCHING THE BROADCAST FROM UNUSUAL PLACES . . .

THOUSANDS OF VIEWERS LIKE HIS INTERVIEWS WITH FAMOUS STARS . . .

THE SHOW TAKES ON ADDED COLOR BECAUSE OF WEIRD GUESTS . . .

MILLIONS OF FANS ENJOY STEVE'S TELEPHONE CALLS . . .

Hello, U.S. Army Recruiting Office? I would like to re-enlist in the army. Name? Steve Allen, 32-43 Walnut Road, Hollywood. Thank you.

Is this Al's meat market? Do you sell fresh buffalo meat? What, What! This is the 56th Street Police Station. er, er. No, no this isn't the Steve Allen show . . . No . . . I'm not trying to be funny . . . Oh, No . . . I just got a ticket for talking back to a policeman!!

Opps! We forgot to pay the telephone bill this month—the phone has been disconnected!

SHOW'S POPULAR BECAUSE OF STEVE'S GREAT COMEDY STYLE . .

This morning a bum stopped me and asked for 25 dollars for a cup of coffee. I told him coffee is only 10 cents a cup and he said I know, but I'm a big tipper!

BEASTYRUST SALE!

Save a big $1.53 on Extra-long sets!

(on extra-short sets for midgets, you save 93c)

5" Longer (All Wood)

Sleep longer. Sleep better. Snore and your old lady makes you sleep in the living room. Save $1.53 or $20. (If you don't want springs in the mattress.) Buy now during our 1,079th Beastyrust sale. (We have more sales than anyone else in the business— gosh, do we like money!) Remember our sale lasts for only two months — August, 1964 and September, 1965.

Here's why ordinary mattresses sag. Too much weight on any area causes a mess. (So next time tell your horse to take his saddle off before he goes to sleep).

Beastyrust coils are made of solid, sharp steel. You won't sag. Matter of fact you won't get too much sleep. Our mattresses are big sellers in India.

BEASTYRUST
$16.50 Extra fern— guaranteed a week
Summons

New free booklet, "How to buy a mattress or "How to count sheep when you can't sleep." Serd name and address to Summons Company, Kreel Mart, Box S-N-O-R-E, Lump, Ill.

71

THE ART

Just as boxers must train—

. . . for the big fight

so lovers must train—

. . . for the big moment

OF KISSING

KISSING CELEBRITIES

BEN CASEY ... famous for his SANITARY KISS

MARCELLO MASTROIANNI
... famous for his fiery KISS OF PASSION

AL CAPONE ... famous for his KISS OF DEATH

SUPERMAN ... famous for his SUPER KISS

A MARTIAN

Dear Mom and Dad:
We landed in a strange-looking place called "Flatbush, Brooklyn." The natives were friendly-except one angry-looking man who was wearing a blue uniform and kept yelling he would give me a ticket for double parking my space ship. (I parked it on top of a bus.)

Later I walked along the street and the natives gave me many funny looks. In fact one native staggered out of a place named "Mike's Bar and Grill" and stared
(cont'd)

When I showed them how we smoke on Mars, they were startled. (I put the cigarette in my left ear and let the smoke come out of my toe nails.)

Another strange thing they do here is to drive on the right side of the road. But get this-their right is our left and so they're really driving backwards.

Their food is yccckko!!! All a woman seems to do to prepare a meal is to take a box out of the refrigerator and place
(cont'd)

HARRY'S OWN SWEET SHOPPE

BRESLIN

EQUAL RIGHTS!
FORMER LANDOWNERS ASSOCIATION
MOHAWK BROOKLYN CHAP. 7

SEVERIN

Writes Home From Earth

at me and then shouted something that sounded like "My gosh, that does it — tomorrow I'm going on the wagon!" Maybe it was the big hat I was wearing at the time — it was the green one with the live Wyyabokine on top.

The inhabitants of this planet have some very weird customs. Like the way they smoke. Here they place a cigarette in their mouth and light it. You have to laugh because it's a very funny sight.

(cont'd)

it in the kitchen stove for a couple of minutes. (I think they call it T.V. Dinners.) And you should see what they do with meatballs. Hold on to your zerlo — they eat them. Hee Hee!!! When I told them we use meatballs for ball bearings in our cars, they laughed like a bunch of crazy people. (Strange, strange folks!)

You should see how the men on this planet shave! Now get this — they shave the hair off their faces from (cont'd)

the outside! That's right — from the outside — not from the inside like the men on Mars.

The natives' music is at least 100 years behind ours. Right now the big rage with teenagers is Rock 'N' Roll. I told them they are not up-to-date and they should get with our music, "THE XSTOEPEX ZUKERDRO FOX-FIP." You know, that dance where we stand on our heads and the room moves around us slowly? (cont'd)

The weather here is real crazy. When it rains, it rains water and not hot chicken soup.

I will write you another letter soon. I think my fountain pen is starting to run out of brink.

your loving daughter,
Zelbazake

P.S. Please send me my Craskzeborez — It's cold here.

GET OUT THE VOTE!

The twenties had their Rudy Vallee adorers; the forties had their Sinatra-worshippers; the fifties had their Presley idolizers. And now CRACKED would like to pay tribute to the fans, who, for sheer enthusiasm and pure hysteria, are without equal. We're referring, of course, to the American girls who worship English recording stars.

SUPER FAN-ELAN

Eye with which she sees eye-to-eye with fellow admirers of the Animals.

Head that can easily be turned by the likes of Peter and Gordon.

Teeth to grind in anger at the policemen who kept her from getting Dave Clark's autograph on his last tour.

Lip which she gave to the hotel doorman who kept her from talking personally to Freddie and the Dreamers.

Neck she'll stick out to defend her idols against Presley and Chuck Berry fans.

Nose to be put to the grindstone for figuring out ways of getting tickets to the next Beatles Concert.

Stomach which can't stomach Frank Sinatra or any of the other old fogies her mother adores.

Heart to love Paul McCartney from the bottom of.

Arm and leg which she'd gladly pay for just one kiss from George Harrison.

Back of the hand she'd like to give to those nasty theater ushers who stopped her from going backstage to see Herman's Hermits.

Hip which she considers herself, coz she digs the Kinks, Hollies and Walker Brothers.

Fingers which she works to the bones to pay for those albums by the Rolling Stones.

Heel for reminding her of the heel of an airport guard who prevented her from grabbing Tom Jones' scarf as a souvenir.

SEVERIN

JAMES BROWN IS OUT OF SIGHT

ANATOMY OF A SUPER FAN

78

Golly! It's tea-time over there now!

Her watch is always set some five hours ahead to London time, so it can beat in time with her English favorite's.

She's never without the latest copy of a British fan magazine which she has flown to her direct from England.

Your brother swiped your diary!

Phew! For a second, I thought it was my copy of "Rave."

While she collects autographs, her real prize is her collection of more tangible souvenirs . . .

LEFT SOCK BELONGING TO CHARLIE WATTS OF THE ROLLING STONES

GRIP HANDLE FROM ON OF OF JOHN LENNON'S SUITCASES

JELLY BEAN WITH WHICH I ACTUALLY HIT PAUL McCARTNEY OF THE BEATLES

FILTER TIP FROM CIGARETTE GEORGE HARRISON SMOKED

COPY OF CRACKED BOUGHT AT KESSLER'S SWEET SHOPPE WHERE I BUY ALL MY FAN MAGS

TOOTHBRUSH BELONGING TO MANFRED MANN

PHONE OVER WHICH RINGO ONCE MADE A CALL

RIGHT SHOE BELONGING TO GARY STEVENS — DEEJAY OF WMCA

wmca good guy

She possesses scale layouts of all the hotels and theaters in town so that she can plot and follow the exact whereabout of any visiting English rockers.

She is thoroughly versed on English affairs:

ENGLISH HISTORY—She knows a wide assortment of historical facts like the exact date the Beatles were awarded their M.B.E. medals.

ENGLISH GEOGRAPHY—She knows all the home addresses and hangouts of her Liverpudlian favorites.

ENGLISH ECONOMICS—She's aware of Britain's chief export (rock 'n' roll records) and Britain's chief import (dollars from American fans).

ENGLISH LANGUAGE—She's very fluent in her ability to translate strange terms like "grotty," "gear," "nit," "daft," "wiggy," etc.

. . . In addition, she holds a Ph.D. Degree (Professor of Hip Discs).

If we storm the hotel lobby en masse, a few of us should make it up to their room.

Synchronize your watches, girls!

309 311 313
307
305
303
301

PROPERTY OF "The Rolling Rocks" FAN CLUB

THE COMPOSITE ENGLISH ROCK AND ROLLER

1. Take the cunning hair style of **PAUL McCARTNEY** (The Beatles)

2. . . . The pop-eyed expression of **PETER NOONE** (Herman's Hermits)

3. . . . The slapping technique of **MICK JAGGER** (Rolling Stones)

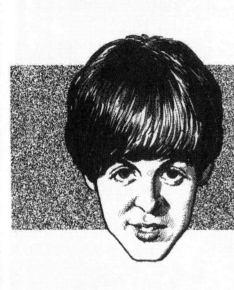  

4. . . . The stylish shirt of **DAVE CLARK** (Dave Clark 5)

5. . . . The zany vitality of **FREDDIE GARRITY** (Freddie & the Dreamers)

6. . . . The surly mouth of **ERIC BURDON** (The Animals)

. . . And then add:

7. All the moodiness of **THE MOODY BLUES . . .**

8. All the flightiness of **THE YARDBIRDS . . .**

9. And all the kinkiness of **THE KINKS!**

PUT THEM ALL TOGETHER AND YOU HAVE . . .

A few weeks ago, after we checked into a room at the Hotel Milton-Flink-Hilton, we got to thinking about what happens to the appearance of a room after different guests have occupied it. CRACKED is proud to present the stirring saga of

ROOM 5C

SIGBJÖRN

(OR HOT AND COLD RUNNING SOMETHING IN EVERY ROOM)

Room 5C—How it looks when it's empty.

Same room after a family of four has spent a week in it.

5C was next rented by a gangster who was hiding from the police.

One of the most popular hobbies in the world is photography. Almost every family owns at least one camera. It's been said that if all the cameras in the world were laid end to end, you'd get one heck of a picture! In keeping with the tremendous popularity of photography, we give you...

A CRACKED LOOK AT PHOTOGRAPHY

TYPES OF CAMERAS:

BOX CAMERA

35MM CAMERA

ULTRA MODERN CAMERA

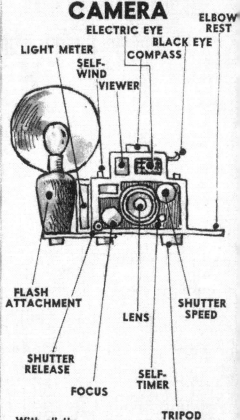

ELECTRIC EYE
ELBOW REST
LIGHT METER
BLACK EYE
COMPASS
SELF-WIND
VIEWER
FLASH ATTACHMENT
LENS
SHUTTER SPEED
SHUTTER RELEASE
SELF-TIMER
FOCUS
TRIPOD ATTACHMENT

BOX CAMERA PICTURE

35MM PICTURES

With all the attachments, we can't afford film!

HOW TO TAKE PROPER PICTURES:

Make sure your camera is loaded.

Get subject in focus.

Make sure your subject is still.

DEVELOPING AND PRINTING:

CHEMICALS . . .

AND EQUIPMENT . . .

PLUS A DARK ROOM.

HOW TO PROPERLY PRINT YOUR PICTURES:

Make sure no light is seeping into your dark room.

OOOOPS! BONK! CRASH!

TINKLE! SPLASH! CRASH! TINKLE! THUMPK! SLOSH!

If you followed all the instructions, your picture should look like this.

For still better results, take pictures to your corner drugstore.

TYPES OF LIGHT METERS:

GERMAN METER

JAPANESE METER

PARKING METER

TYPES OF FILM:

SLOW

MEDIUM

FAST
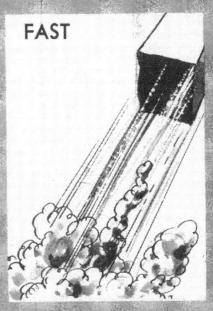

TYPES OF FLASHES:

BULB

NO! THIS IS NOT FRANKENSTEIN'S MONSTER....ED.

LIGHTNING

THIS IS!...ED.

GORDON

HERE ARE SOME SPECIALIZED CAMERAS:

CHEESECAKE CAMERA

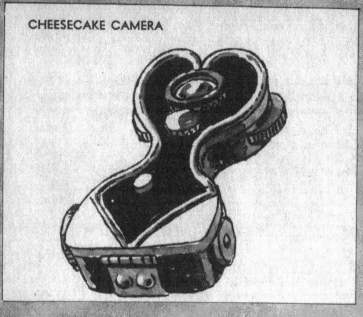

ACTION SHOTS CAMERA

NO ARTICLE ON PHOTOGRAPHY WOULD BE COMPLETE WITHOUT A PHOTO CONTEST

"SNOW," taken by Billy Furd,
age 1½. (f-30, speed—65 m.p.h.).

"AT WORK," taken by Arnie
Creelpotski, coal miner.

"CLEO," taken by Joseph Manckowitz and D. F. Zanuck on 73¼mm., with
a TED-I-O lens, Super PANAFONY Sound, and $3,500,000.67 worth of film.

THE CONDEMNED MAN

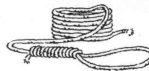

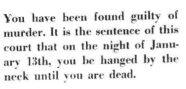

You have been found guilty of murder. It is the sentence of this court that on the night of January 13th, you be hanged by the neck until you are dead.

Squares! Fools! Do they really think they can kill Dr. Bonerath?

Igor, before they hang me tonight, I will take my secret LXD formula . . . with iron!

Yes, master.

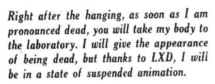

Right after the hanging, as soon as I am pronounced dead, you will take my body to the laboratory. I will give the appearance of being dead, but thanks to LXD, I will be in a state of suspended animation.

Now, pay close attention. At exactly 3:15, you are to administer 5c.c. of the LXD antidote. The slightest mistake will be fatal!

Do you have it straight?

Yes, master. At 3:15 . . .

The visitor must leave!

Ah . . . At 4:15, 3c.c. No, that's not right . . . Uh, 4c.c. at 4 o'clock . . . Uh, master?

Visiting hours are over!

91

The average person in the course of an average day must be hit by at least five or six cliches —enough to cause a slight headache. We at CRACKED have started a campaign to give all the cliche-sufferers a chance to fight back with some fast answers by making use of . . .

Cracked's Snappy Comebacks!

SEVERIN

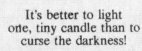

...AND CRACKED'S FAMOUS JANITOR, SYLVESTER P. SMYTHE, SAYS . . .

There's a recent war movie out that didn't have the usual loud sounds of war-like bombs and artillery to irritate you. Instead, the script dealt with the relationship of two enemy soldiers stranded together on an island during World War II and their struggle to survive. (Come to think of it, the movie needs some bombs and artillery to keep you awake!) The movie opens as the American Marine, played by Lee Marvin, finds himself washed up on the island. With an incredible cool and nerves of steel, he calmly throws back his head and yells as loud as he can...

WROTE BY STU SCHWARTZBERG — DRAWED BY EDVARD SEVERIN

98

102

AFTERWORD by Mort Todd

Hope you enjoyed *The Comedy Art of John Severin*, culled from the 1950s & 60s and showcasing one of the greatest American illustrators ever born! I had the extreme honor and pleasure of working with John as an editor, writer and penciler for almost 25 years, starting at *Cracked* and on to Marvel Comics, advertising and our newspaper comic strip *Celebrity Biografix*. His incredible talent has awed, amused and inspired generations of readers.

According to John, this prolific genius of the art world was hatched on December 25, 1921 (though biographies often note the 26th). He said this resulted in him getting shortchanged when it came to getting separate birthday and Christmas gifts! John's art skills were self taught, and as the preceding pages will attest, he was in command of a great variety of illustrating styles and techniques.

By the time he was 11 years old, John's cartoons were appearing in *The Hobo News*, an early "street newspaper." His first comic book work was a crime story for a title published by the famous Joe Simon and Jack Kirby team in 1947. John quickly moved on to become writer, editor and artist on many western comics, like *American Eagle* and *Black Bull*, which his friend Will Elder also collaborated on.

Severin's art was very sharp and recognizable by the time he was working for the legendary EC Comics in the 1950s. He gained fame for his meticulous attention to detail and accuracy. He edited *Two-Fisted Tales* as well as contributing art to that and *Frontline Combat*. He also co-founded *Mad* with editor Harvey Kurtzman at EC and worked on its earliest issues when it was still a comic book.

After EC went out of business in 1955, John's work appeared in a variety of publishers' releases, like at Stan Lee's Atlas Comics as it morphed into Marvel Comics. There he did more western and war comics, as well as *The Incredible Hulk, Sgt. Fury* and *Nick Fury, Agent of S.H.I.E.L.D*. At Charlton Comics he did a run on *Billy the Kid*, which has recently been collected. He's also whipped up some way-out and weird horror stories for Harvey Comics, Warren's *Creepy* and *Eerie, Help!* and *Cracked's For Monsters Only!* and *Monsters Attack!* In all, during the 1950s and 1960s, while working on the very pages in this volume, John is estimated to have drawn some amazing 100 pages (and some paintings) a month!

John's sister, Marie Severin, is also a well-known artist and they united on a few stories for *Cracked*, such as the LBJ *Lone Rancher* story she penciled in this book, that John inked. Marie was also a veteran member of Marvel Comics' infamous bullpen and provided many cover sketches for other artists to follow and art corrections. She contributed many pages of comics herself there, including a Severin siblings collaboration on the the barbarian series, *Kull*. She is famous for her coloring of the original EC Comics and their reprints, and it's a little known fact that John himself was colorblind. That might explain why, over the course of painting hundreds of covers for *Cracked*, sometimes flames, E.T. or Freddy Krueger would appear green.

Conservatively, John easily illustrated thousands of pages for *Cracked* since the first issue in 1958. His long run would only be interrupted for a couple issues in 1985 when new publishers took over the title and he had a disagreement with the new editor. I was hired, at first, as a creative consulting editor and the first thing I told the publishers was that *Cracked* would soon die without the Severin powerhouse at the graphic helm. My first mandate was to get John back at any cost and I *did*. It began a long creative collaboration that lasted many years and culminated with our *Celebrity Biographix* comic strip. I wrote and did layouts and John's immense talent crafted the astonishing likenesses of hundreds of famous people and their life stories in nine panels. One of my greatest publishing regrets is that Marvel Comics never published an Elvis Presley series we worked on together.

John continued at *Cracked* after I left the magazine, until new publishers again thought they could do without his talent… and *Cracked* **died** (only to live on as a ghost of itself on the internet). John went on to create extraordinary artwork for war, western and adventure stories at Marvel, DC Comics and Dark Horse Comics, right up to his passing at 90 in 2012.

Many awards were garnered by John in the comics industry, ranging from an Inkpot Award in 1998, the Cartoon Art Museum's Sparky Award in 2001, and he was inducted into the Will Eisner Award Hall of Fame in 2003. His magnificent body of work will continue to awe, amuse and inspire future generations of artists and readers, and we hope you enjoy this slice of his career from *Cracked's* first ten years. Some of the material may not be considered "PC" in this day and age, but consider, for historical reasons, its worth. You almost have to be a professional cultural historian (aka *geek*) of mid-20th century media and politics to understand many of the references in these pages, but there's no denying John's work makes it fun as heck!

Mort Todd is a writer, illustrator, editor, publisher, animator and film maker. He is known for his *Back from the Grave* CD covers, was editor-in-chief of *Cracked*, created *Monsters Attack!* and launched the Marvel Music line of comics. He is currently releasing the Charlton Neo comics line along with other publications at *morttodd.com*

BIBLIOGRAPHY

Note: Early issues of *Cracked* did not credit creators in the stories, but did list them on the contents page. However, editor Paul Laikin did write a lot of the early stories presented here. It is also pretty apparent that prolific *Cracked* writer George Gladir wrote *Super Fan-Elan* among others, and that Stu Schwartzberg wrote and did lay-outs for *Help! I'm in the Pacific!* ---Mort Todd

Original cover art for *Cracked* Mazagine #13 (March 1960) by **John Severin**.

Original cover art for *Cracked* Mazagine #23 (February 1962) by **John Severin.**

Made in the USA
Las Vegas, NV
03 May 2024